CW00841942

Pinny and the Bird

Peter Firmin

ANDRE DEUTSCH

For Melanie and Laurence

First published in 1985 by
André Deutsch Limited
105 Great Russell Street London WC1B 3LJ

Copyright © 1985 by Peter Firmin
All rights reserved

British Library Cataloguing in Publication Data

Firmin, Peter
  Pinny and the bird.
  I. Title
  823'.914[J]   PZ7

  ISBN 0-233-97815-1

In a little china house on a shelf
in the sitting room, lives a tiny
wooden doll, no taller than a pin,
and her name is Pinny.

Pinny can walk and move her arms,
and even bend her knees and elbows.
Her dress is a scrap of orange silk
and her shoes are tiny dabs of red paint.

Next to the china house is a little
sailing boat. A wooden sailor sits
in the boat. He wears a painted blue
suit and a yellow straw hat.
His name is Victor.

The girl who plays in the sitting room
is called Jo. One day she played with
the house and left it on the carpet.
Pinny looked out of her door.
She couldn't see Victor or his boat.
Where could he be?

The boy who plays with the boat
is called Tom. Perhaps he had left
the boat outside.

Pinny went to look for Victor in the
hall. Just at that moment, somebody
opened the door to the kitchen.

A gust of wind blew Pinny out through
the gap under the front door.

The wind tumbled Pinny over the doorstep and dropped her halfway down the garden path, where a thrush was scratching around, looking for twigs for her nest.

The thrush pecked at Pinny thinking she was a twig.
She picked Pinny up in her beak, and flew up to her nest in a tall tree.

The thrush poked Pinny into the prickly nest and flew away.
Pinny struggled out and looked down. It was a tall tree and she was rather frightened. Then she saw a feather, and had a clever idea.

Pinny climbed on to the feather.
She shuffled it nearer, and nearer
to the edge of the nest, until
suddenly it tipped up and slid off.
Pinny and the feather were falling.

Down she went; down, down, floating through the air. It was a little bit frightening but she was brave and held on tightly.

Some swallows swooped very near but they were only catching flies.

The feather landed on the pond, quite softly, so that Pinny did not get at all wet. Across the water she saw a little boat stuck fast in the reeds.
Victor was standing in it waving his arms.

"Help, help!" he called. "Save me. My boat is stuck and it won't move." Pinny dipped her hands in the water and paddled over to the boat. "Don't be afraid," she said. "We can paddle ashore on my feather."

Victor climbed on to the feather. Together they paddled hard and soon reached the shore. They scrambled up the bank and ran up the garden path.

Pinny and Victor crept in under the front door and ran along the hall. The china house was still on the carpet. They were just in time to run inside before Jo came in to put it back on the shelf.

Tom couldn't remember where he had left the boat.

The next day he found it on the pond but Victor was not in it.

They looked everywhere and when at last they found him with Pinny in her house, they were so pleased that they never thought to wonder how he got there.

Tom put Victor back in his boat on
the shelf next to the house.

"It was lucky we found them," he said.

"Something terrible might have happened."